LINEUP FOR YESTERDAY

LINE UP FOR

Creative 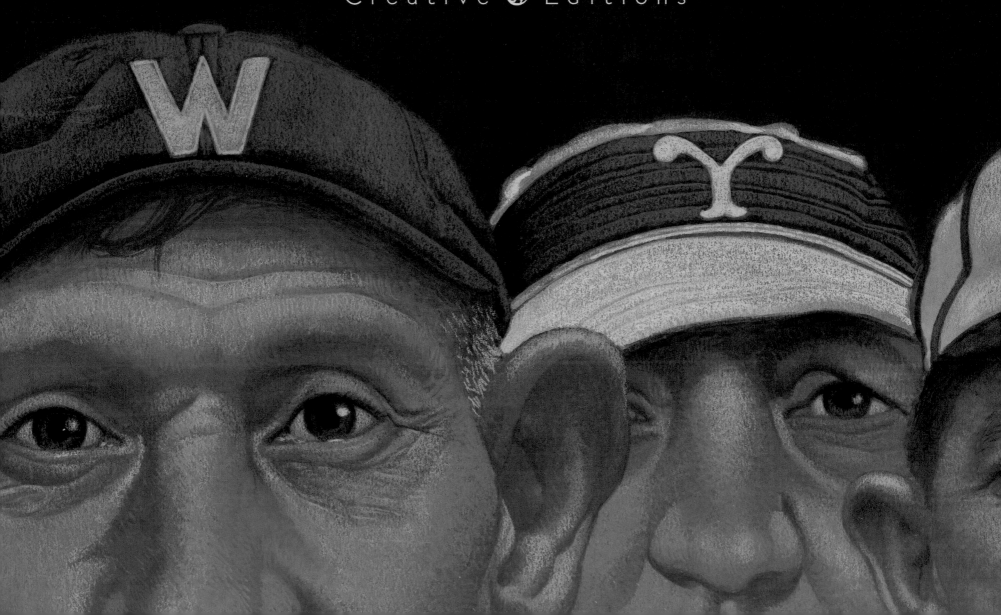 Editions

YESTERDAY

OGDEN NASH

illustrated by C. F. PAYNE

Once upon a Time...

My father, Ogden Nash, grew up in Rye, New York, in the early 1900s. My grandfather made a point of taking him to all the baseball games he could in the area, even when my father was supposed to stay at home in bed with a summer cold. It was then that my father's passionate love of the game was born—a love that ended only with his death in 1971.

I shall always remember the hot summer days of my own childhood spent with my father at old Oriole Park in the early 1940s. The crunch of peanut shells between my fingers, the sing-song calls of the vendors, the hot dogs that tasted better than any other hot dogs, and at last the staccato cry of "Play ball!" The Nashes were avid fans of Jack Dunn's International League Orioles, and we were ecstatic when they won the "Little World Series" in 1944. We always sat on the first base side, a lineup of Nashes— my father, my sister Isabel, me, and my mother Frances. Both my parents kept score faithfully and taught Isabel and me the intricacies of doing so ourselves. I still equate

Tinker to Evers to Chance with 6-4-3, and the letter "K" will always remind me of Casey's disastrous third strike.

Dad told Isabel and me many tales of the famous players of old, some of whom appear in "Lineup." We especially liked the Orioles players he described—Wee Willie Keeler and his teammates Hughie Jennings and John McGraw, Wilbert Robinson, and Roger Bresnahan—and the immortal Babe Ruth, a Baltimore native. All of the names in "Lineup" are wonderfully familiar to me. The only player not in the Hall of Fame is Bobo Newsom, and I'm sure Dad would think this an oversight. He loved "Ol' Bobo" and believed that, in his case, eccentricity overshadowed very real talent, leading many to undervalue Newsom's career.

Many years later, after my father's death, Mother would look forward to Larry King's annual recitation of "Lineup for Yesterday" on late-night radio at the opening of each baseball season. When I read the "Lineup" poems now, I can find myself for a moment back at old Oriole Park on a golden summer day. I can hear the crack of a bat, the hush of expectation before the roar of the crowd, and my father yelling "Yay-ay-ay-ay!" as he jumps up to cheer the man on third home.

–Linell Nash Smith

A is for Alex
The great Alexander;
More Goose eggs he pitched
Than a popular gander.

★ Grover Cleveland Alexander
Position: Pitcher   Major-League Seasons: 1911–30
Teams: Philadelphia Phillies, Chicago Cubs,
St. Louis Cardinals
Batted: Right   Threw: Right
Height: 6-foot-1   Weight: 185 pounds
Career Numbers: 373 wins, 208 losses, 2.56 ERA

B is for Bresnahan
Back of the plate;
The Cubs were his love,
And McGraw his hate.

⭐ Roger Philip Bresnahan
Position: Catcher   Major-League Seasons: 1897, 1900–15
Teams: Washington Senators, Chicago Orphans/Cubs,
Baltimore Orioles, New York Giants, St. Louis Cardinals
Batted: Right   Threw: Right
Height: 5-foot-9   Weight: 200 pounds
Career Numbers: .279 BA, 26 HR, 530 RBI

C is for Cobb,
Who grew spikes and
    not corn,
And made all the basemen
Wish they weren't born.

★ Tyrus Raymond Cobb
Position: Center Fielder
Major-League Seasons: 1905–28
Teams: Detroit Tigers, Philadelphia Athletics
Batted: Left   Threw: Right
Height: 6-foot-1   Weight: 175 pounds
Career Numbers: .366 BA, 117 HR, 1,938 RBI

Known as "Alex" or "Pete," **Grover Cleveland Alexander** was among 13 children born on a Nebraska farm, and long days of shucking corn gave him a powerful right wrist. He used that wrist to become a pitching star for the Philadelphia Phillies. Off the mound, Alexander did not look the part. His uniform and cap never quite fitted his gangly frame correctly.

He seldom spoke, and when he did, it was in a small, whispery voice. On the hill, though, he was nothing short of masterful, slinging lively fastballs and a wicked curve with an effortless motion. As a rookie, Alex won 28 games.

In 1917, the Phillies traded Alexander to the Chicago Cubs, and in 1918, he was shipped off to the battlefields of World War I as an artillery officer. While in France, his pitching arm was damaged firing howitzers, and a shell exploded near his head, deafening him in his left ear and apparently triggering the onset of epilepsy. To help cope with those injuries and the haunting memories of combat, he turned increasingly to alcohol. Amazingly, Alexander returned to baseball seemingly unaffected, putting up a 1.72 earned run average (ERA) in 1919—a Cubs record that still stands.

Epilepsy and alcoholism eventually slowed Alexander, and in 1926, he was traded in midseason to the St. Louis Cardinals. Still, "Alexander the Great" had one last moment of triumph in him. The Cardinals met the New York Yankees in the 1926 World Series. Alexander won Game 6 for the Redbirds. Then, in the deciding Game 7, the Cardinals' starting pitcher vacated the mound in the seventh inning with the bases loaded, two out, and St. Louis up 3–2. Cardinals manager Rogers Hornsby called on the 39-year-old Alex, who—in a performance that made him a St. Louis legend—

struck out slugger Tony Lazzeri on four knee-high pitches and then held the Yankees hitless for two more innings to give St. Louis the championship.

Alexander lived the rest of his days in virtual poverty, and while he was able to attend the ceremony for his 1938 induction into the Baseball Hall of Fame at Cooperstown, New York, he said sadly a few years later, "I'm in the Hall of Fame, and I'm proud to be there, but I can't eat the Hall of Fame."

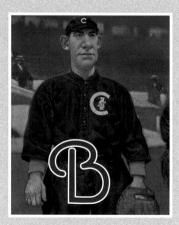

Roger Bresnahan was known for three things: his versatility, his creativity, and his temper. Nicknamed "The Duke of Tralee" on account of his Irish heritage (Tralee being a prominent Irish town), Bresnahan displayed the first by putting in time at every position on the field early in his big-league career. Finally, in 1905, he settled in at catcher for the New York Giants, pairing up with pitcher Christy Mathewson to form one of the most renowned batteries in baseball history. For several seasons, Bresnahan's tremendous hitting and surprising speed made him the rare catcher to bat leadoff.

It was in New York, too, that Bresnahan demonstrated his creativity. Legendary Giants skipper John McGraw once called Bresnahan the smartest player he ever managed. The backstop earned such praise by developing new catching techniques such as the snap throw to first and the slide step to block the plate from runners coming home. He also was a pioneer in the invention of protective gear. After a head-high beaning put him in the hospital, he devised the batting helmet and soon was showing up at the ballpark with shinguards, a chest protector, and a padded catcher's mask as well. The Duke was initially mocked by his peers for these innovations, but within a few years, the new equipment began to be adopted sport-wide.

Like McGraw, Bresnahan had a short fuse, which was lit often after he joined the Cardinals in 1909 as a player/manager. That Irish temper—which could be directed at teammates, opponents, and umpires with equal fury—ensured a brief stay in St. Louis. The story goes that, after a Cardinals loss to the Cubs, new team owner Helene Britton criticized Bresnahan's judgment on a play. The Duke stormed off, declaring, "No woman can tell me how to play a ball game!" He was soon sold to the Cubs, for whom he played his final three seasons.

Ty Cobb was surly, hostile, and always seemed to have at least two chips on his shoulder. His playing style was so aggressive that the *Detroit Free Press* described it as "daring to the point of dementia." Probably the most disliked man in baseball in his day, "The Georgia Peach" nevertheless commanded respect from all in the game. His base running was nothing short of phenomenal. He stole home 50 times, a record that will probably stand forever. Six times, after reaching first base, he proceeded to steal second, then third, then home, often coming hard into each base—and the baseman—with cleats he had deliberately sharpened. Athletics manager Connie Mack warned his players, "Never get Mr. Cobb angry."

In 1912, a heckler in New York's Highland Park did just that, blistering Cobb's ears every time he came to bat. By the sixth inning, Cobb could stand no more and vaulted into the stands to attack the fan, giving him a thorough drubbing despite discovering that the man had no hands, having lost them in an industrial accident. American League president Ban Johnson, who was in attendance, immediately suspended Cobb. His Tigers teammates went on strike in protest the next day. Cobb urged them back to the field after one game, but the incident helped spur the formation of a players' union, which gave ballplayers greater bargaining power in dealing with team owners.

As a player, Cobb's drive for perfection was so intense that, although he threw right-handed, he taught himself to bat left-handed in order to start out one step closer to first base. Such commitment made Cobb second only to Babe Ruth on the roster of early baseball greats—and some rank him above even the Babe. The Georgia Peach set so many records during his 24-year career that some, including his .366 career batting average, still stand.

D is for Dean,

The grammatical Diz,
When they asked,
 Who's the tops?
Said correctly, I is.

★ Jay Hanna Dean
Position: Pitcher   Major-League Seasons: 1930–41, 1947
Teams: St. Louis Cardinals, Chicago Cubs, St. Louis Browns
Batted: Right   Threw: Right
Height: 6-foot-2   Weight: 182 pounds
Career Numbers: 150 wins, 83 losses, 3.02 ERA

★ John Joseph Evers
Position: Second Baseman   Major-League Seasons: 1902–17,
1922, 1929   Teams: Chicago Orphans/Cubs, Boston
Braves, Philadelphia Phillies, Chicago White Sox
Batted: Left   Threw: Right
Height: 5-foot-9   Weight: 125 pounds
Career Numbers: .270 BA, 12 HR, 538 RBI

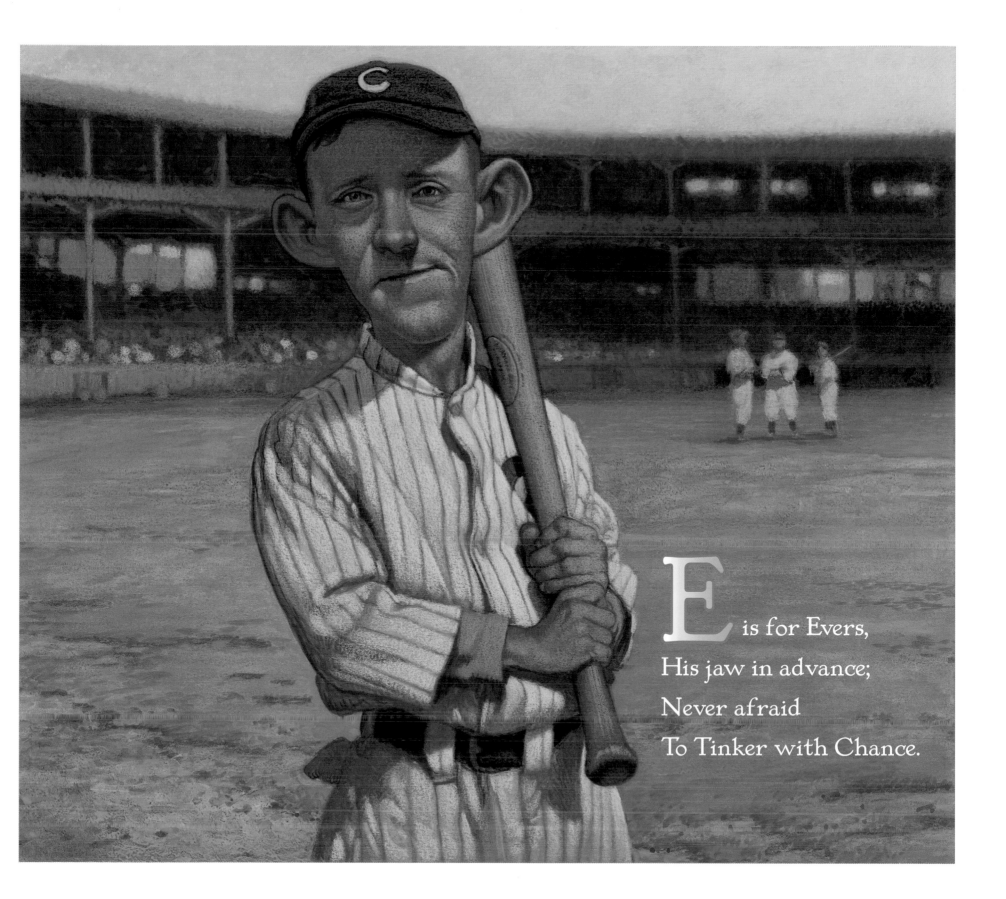

E is for Evers,
His jaw in advance;
Never afraid
To Tinker with Chance.

F is for Fordham
And Frankie and Frisch;
I wish he were back
With the Giants, I wish.

★ Frank Francis Frisch
Positions: Second Baseman, Manager
Major-League Seasons: 1919–37 (as player);
1933–38, 1940–46, 1949–51 (as manager)
Teams: New York Giants, St. Louis Cardinals,
Pittsburgh Pirates, Chicago Cubs
Batted: Left and Right   Threw: Right
Height: 5-foot-11   Weight: 165 pounds
Career Numbers: .316 BA, 105 HR, 1,244 RBI
Managerial Numbers: 1,138 wins, 1,078 losses,
1 world championship

G is for Gehrig,
The Pride of the Stadium;
His record pure gold,
His courage, pure radium.

★ Henry Louis Gehrig
Position: First Baseman
Major-League Seasons: 1923–39
Team: New York Yankees
Batted: Left   Threw: Left
Height: 6 feet   Weight: 200 pounds
Career Numbers: .340 BA, 493 HR, 1,995 RBI

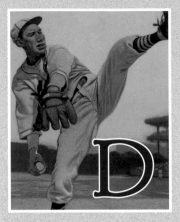

For a Baseball Hall-of-Famer, **Dizzy Dean** had a short career. He played his first major-league game in 1930 with the Cardinals and his last true game in 1941 with the Cubs. But he accomplished more in his first eight seasons than most pitchers do in a lifetime. And Dean did it with memorable, linguistic flair. His witticisms were as quoted in Depression-era America as Yankees great Yogi Berra's are today. For example, once, upon being released from the hospital after a serious beaning, Dean announced, "They X-rayed my head and found nothing."

From 1932 to 1935, Dizzy led the National League in strikeouts every year. His best season was 1934, when he led the Cardinals to the World Series championship. Known as much for his braggadocio as his pitching, Dean had predicted that he and his brother Paul (called "Daffy"), also a hurler for the Cards, would win 45 games for the team that year; in fact, they won a combined 49, with Dizzy laying claim to 30. As Dizzy was fond of saying, "It ain't bragging if ya can back it up."

In the 1937 All-Star Game, Dizzy was struck by a line drive and suffered a broken toe. The injury forced him to alter his pitching motion, which in turn damaged his arm, and he retired in 1941. Six years later, he was working as a radio broadcaster for the St. Louis Browns. After witnessing several frustrating pitching performances by the team, Dizzy blustered on air, "Doggone it, I can pitch better than 9 out of 10 guys on this staff!" The Browns took him up on it and asked him to pitch four innings of the last game of the season. Dizzy rose to the occasion, allowing no runs and hitting a single in his only at bat.

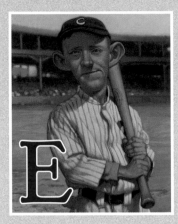

Johnny Evers entered the majors in September 1902 with the Chicago Orphans (soon to be renamed the Cubs). Nicknamed "The Crab" because of the way he sidled up to grounders, Evers formed the middle part of a double-play trio—along with shortstop Joe Tinker and first baseman Frank Chance—that was immortalized by New York newspaperman Franklin P. Adams in a famous rhyme:

> These are the saddest of possible words:
> Tinker to Evers to Chance.
> Trio of bear cubs, and fleeter than birds,
> Tinker to Evers to Chance.
> Ruthlessly pricking our gonfalon bubble,
> Making a Giant hit into a double—
> Words that are heavy with nothing but trouble:
> Tinker to Evers to Chance.

If not the shortest man to gain induction into the Hall of Fame, Evers was almost certainly the slightest, barely tipping the scales at 100 pounds as a rookie (though a love of chocolate helped bulk him up to 125). But the nimble second baseman was heavy on combativeness. Sportswriter Fred Lieb once called him a "truculent little gladiator who packed more aggressiveness in his frame than any other player of his size."

Evers played big in big moments; he batted .350 in both the 1907 and 1908 World Series for the Cubs and upped his average to .438 in the 1914 Series as a member of the Boston Braves. That 1914 season proved to be the Crab's last great hurrah. As he set a big-league record by getting thrown out of nine games, the feisty second baseman took Boston from last place to first in the final 10 weeks of the season, then helped the Braves sweep the Athletics in the World Series.

Frankie Frisch starred in four sports while attending New York's Fordham University. He captained the baseball, football, and basketball teams and also excelled in track, from which he earned his nickname, "The Fordham Flash." Frisch joined the New York Giants in 1919 and by 1920 was not only the starting second baseman but team captain.

In both 1921 and 1922, the Flash's competitive fire helped drive the Giants to victory in the World Series. Frisch was a go-for-broke player with spectacular speed and a fearsome bat. However, those traits were accompanied by a quick temper that eventually collided with fiery Giants manager John McGraw, and in 1926, Frisch was traded to St. Louis. There, he headed up the rough and rowdy "Gashouse Gang"—which included the Dean brothers (pitchers Dizzy and Daffy), outfielders Joe "Ducky" Medwick and Pepper Martin, and shortstop Leo Durocher—and led the Cards to world championships in 1931 and 1934.

As a player and manager, Frisch was exceptionally aggressive. He had a talent for umpire-baiting, which got him tossed from many a game. In 1954, after he had retired, Frisch lamented that "rampaging, dictatorial managers have vanished with the bunny hug and the hip flask. Gone are the feuds, fines, profanity, and fun." Yet for all his bluster and fireworks on the field, at home Frisch was a gentle soul who loved classical music, gardening, and dogs. In 1948, he made his way back to New York when Durocher became manager of the Giants and hired him as a coach. As a result of this move, Ogden Nash added the following to his original "Lineup" verse for Frisch:

P.S. Thanks to Durocher,
Now everything's kosher.

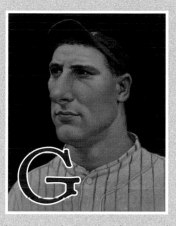

Lou Gehrig became a permanent member of the New York Yankees' lineup in 1925, making his debut as a pinch hitter on June 1. He would play in every Yankees game for the next 14 years, appearing in 2,130 consecutive games—a record that would stand for 56 years. By 1927, Gehrig was batting cleanup for the Yankees, following Babe Ruth in a lineup so daunting it became known as "Murderers' Row."

Gehrig was a manager's dream, a quiet, unassuming man who could be counted on day after day, year after year. Sportswriter Jim Murray referred to him as "Gibraltar in cleats," and he became popularly known as "The Iron Horse." Gehrig built a career batting average of .340, but in 1938, his production began to tail off. In 1939, after a dismal start, he took himself out of the lineup on May 2. "I haven't been a bit of good to the team since the season started," he told reporters. "It would not be fair to the boys ... or to the baseball public for me to try going on." His dramatic decline was soon explained when he was diagnosed with the incurable disease amyotrophic lateral sclerosis, which would be known ever after as "Lou Gehrig's Disease."

July 4, 1939, was proclaimed "Lou Gehrig Appreciation Day" at Yankee Stadium. It was then and there that Gehrig brought a tear to the eye of every person in attendance, giving the speech that is remembered for the words, "Today, I consider myself the luckiest man on the face of the earth."

The Iron Horse died 2 years later, just shy of his 38th birthday.

H is for Hornsby;

When pitching to Rog,
The pitcher would pitch,
Then the pitcher would dodge.

★ Rogers Hornsby
Position: Second Baseman
Major-League Seasons: 1915–37
Teams: St. Louis Cardinals, New York Giants, Boston
Braves, Chicago Cubs, St. Louis Browns
Batted: Right   Threw: Right
Height: 5-foot-11   Weight: 175 pounds
Career Numbers: .358 BA, 301 HR, 1,584 RBI

I is for me,
Not a hard-hitting man,
But an outstanding all-time
Incurable fan.

★ Frederick Ogden Nash
Position: Outfielder, Fan
Lived: August 19, 1902–May 19, 1971
Batted: Right   Threw: Right   Wrote: Right
Height: 6 feet
Playing Weight: 160 pounds
Writing Weight: 180 pounds

J is for Johnson

The Big Train in his prime
Was so fast he could throw
Three strikes at a time.

★ Walter Perry Johnson
Position: Pitcher   Major-League Seasons: 1907–27
Team: Washington Senators
Batted: Right   Threw: Right
Height: 6-foot-1   Weight: 200 pounds
Career Numbers: 417 wins, 279 losses, 2.17 ERA

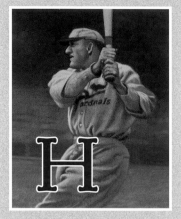

Earning his nickname "The Rajah" by way of his contentious and supremely confident persona, **Rogers Hornsby** set so many batting records that it's hard to count them. He led the National League in slugging nine times, a record that still stands, and his lifetime batting average of .358 remains the highest in NL history. In 1922, he became the only player ever to hit more than 40 home runs and bat over .400 in the same year. His .424 average during the 1924 season has never been equaled.

Baseball was Hornsby's life. To keep fit, he neither smoked nor drank, and to preserve his keen batting eye, he would not watch a movie or even read a newspaper. "People ask me what I do in winter when there's no baseball," he once said. "I'll tell you what I do. I stare out the window and wait for spring." While remembered primarily for his slugging power, the Rajah was also exceptionally fast, which contributed greatly to his 1,011 career extra-base hits.

In addition to his gunfighter's gaze and lively legs, Hornsby was known for his curmudgeonly personality; in fact, some said his meanness was rivaled only by Ty Cobb's. That prickliness resulted in his being frequently traded. In 1926, he was sent to the Giants in a deal for Frankie Frisch, and he would change teams another four times after that. But through those moves, and even in retirement, the Rajah never lost his cocky brand of self-confidence. In a 1962 interview, he was asked how he would fare if he stepped into the batter's box against the modern generation of pitchers. Hornsby thought about it and replied, "I guess I'd hit about .280 or .290." When the interviewer asked "Why so low?", he answered, "Well, I'm 66 years old, what do you expect?"

Ogden Nash played baseball only through his high school years, but his love of the game lasted a lifetime. His favorite team was the New York Giants of Polo Grounds fame, and his favorite player was right fielder Mel Ott. Tremendously saddened when the Giants' owner, Horace Stoneham, moved the team from the Polo Grounds to San Francisco in 1957, Nash wrote:

> The candle's out, the game is up;
> Who has heart for a stirrup cup?
> Farewell Giants and Horace Stoneham
> *De mortuis nil nisi bonum.**

Nash remained a baseball diehard as he earned a living as a poet and lyricist. On August 19, 2002, he joined 12 of the players featured in "Lineup" in being honored by the U.S. Postal Service. An Ogden Nash postage stamp was issued commemorating what would have been his 100th birthday. The stamp featured an image of the poet and the full text of six of his poems, making it literally the smallest collection of poetry ever printed.

* *Say nothing but good of the dead*

Tall and lanky, with remarkably long arms, **Walter Johnson** was nicknamed "The Big Train" due to the locomotive-like steam of his fastball. He delivered that heater using a sidearm, slingshot motion that baffled many a batsman. Once, an opposing hitter left the batter's box after watching Johnson's first two pitches sizzle past for strikes. When the umpire reminded him he had one strike left, the batter replied, "I know it. You can have the next one. It won't do me any good."

Johnson pitched for an often dismal team, the Washington Senators, yet he persevered, working to maintain the very highest level of play every time he took the hill. In his 21 years with the Senators, he hurled 110 shutouts, a record that still stands. For 10 straight seasons, he won 20 or more games despite often receiving little run support from his teammates. At times, it seemed only Babe Ruth and Ty Cobb were a match for him at the plate. But even Cobb was awed. "The first time I faced him, I watched him take that easy windup," Cobb said. "And then something went past me that made me flinch. The thing just hissed with danger. We couldn't touch him ... every one of us knew we'd met the most powerful arm ever turned loose in a ballpark."

Finally, in 1924, the Senators fielded a team that was worthy of Johnson. Going 23–7 that season, Johnson powered the club to its first pennant. Then, in a World Series that went a full seven games against the Giants, he appeared in relief in Game 7. The Big Train held New York scoreless for 4 innings until a Senators grounder in the 12th inning brought a run home, breaking a 3–3 tie and giving Washington the championship.

Johnson retired as a player after the 1927 season and tried his hand at managing, but he proved a mediocre skipper. The consensus view was that he was too gentle and kindly a man to properly command a team. Johnson was among the five players (with Ty Cobb, Christy Mathewson, Babe Ruth, and Honus Wagner) that made up the inaugural class of Hall of Fame inductees in 1936.

K is for Keeler,
As fresh as green paint,
The fastest and mostest
To hit where they ain't.

★ William Henry Keeler
Position: Right Fielder   Major-League Seasons: 1892–1910
Teams: New York Giants, Brooklyn Grooms/Superbas,
Baltimore Orioles, New York Highlanders
Batted: Left   Threw: Left
Height: 5-foot-4   Weight: 140 pounds
Career Numbers: .341 BA, 33 HR, 810 RBI

★ Napoleon Lajoie
Position: Second Baseman   Major-League Seasons: 1896–1916
Teams: Philadelphia Phillies, Philadelphia Athletics,
Cleveland Bronchos/Naps
Batted: Right   Threw: Right
Height: 6-foot-1   Weight: 195 pounds
Career Numbers: .338 BA, 82 HR, 1,599 RBI

L is for Lajoie,
Whom Clevelanders love,
Napoleon himself,
With glue in his glove.

M is for Matty,
Who carried a charm
In the form of an extra
Brain in his arm.

★ Christopher Mathewson
Position: Pitcher
Major-League Seasons: 1900–16
Teams: New York Giants, Cincinnati Reds
Batted: Right   Threw: Right
Height: 6-foot-1   Weight: 195 pounds
Career Numbers: 373 wins, 188 losses, 2.13 ERA

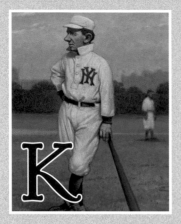

"Wee Willie" Keeler's diminutive stature gave him a catchy nickname, but as Boston Red Sox great Ted Williams once said, "He may have been small in size, but he was huge with the bat."

Keeler broke into the major leagues with the Giants, but his career took off when the Orioles acquired him in 1894. In Baltimore, Keeler blossomed into an extraordinary batsman and coined a memorable phrase through his simple advice on hitting: "Keep your eye on the ball and hit 'em where they ain't." He pioneered what came to be called the "Baltimore chop"—a ball hit hard into the dirt at such a sharp angle that it would bounce high in the air, giving a swift runner the chance to reach base before the ball could be fielded and thrown to first. Keeler had more than enough speed to capitalize on the Baltimore chop, and in 1897, his fleet feet helped him assemble a 44-game hitting streak.

Keeler was credited with perfecting the hit-and-run, the double steal, and, some say, the suicide squeeze. The legend for this last accomplishment goes that Keeler was at bat with a man—Highlanders teammate Jack Chesbro—on third. Suddenly, Chesbro broke to steal home, surprising Keeler and prompting him to stab his bat out at the pitch. The ball fell safely between the pitcher and third baseman while Chesbro scored and Keeler reached first. When the manager later asked Keeler why he hit the ball, he replied, "I didn't see what else there was for me to do to prevent Chesbro from committing suicide."

Napoleon Lajoie (*lah-ZHWAH*) was one of few men ever to have a big-league team named after him. Whether in the field or at the plate, the strapping second baseman cut an impressive and graceful figure. A New York newspaper described him as "living poetry at second base…. A big, swarthy jungle cat whose superiority oozes from him." Lajoie started out with the Philadelphia Phillies and Athletics before being swapped to the Cleveland Bronchos in 1901. There he buoyed a slumping team and was promptly named its captain. At the end of the 1902 season, the Bronchos became the "Naps" in his honor (remaining so for 12 seasons before becoming the Indians).

Lajoie won the American League batting title four times. The last time, in 1910, he made major headlines. America was fixated that summer on his ongoing rivalry with Tigers star Ty Cobb, who had come up to the majors in 1905 and begun challenging Lajoie's hitting records. The Chalmers Auto Company initiated a contest between Lajoie and Cobb, offering a new car to the player with the highest batting average at the end of the regular season. Cobb was ahead in "The Chalmers Race" going into the final two games of the season and sat them out, protecting his average. Lajoie faced long odds in catching his rival, but due to Cobb's general unpopularity among his fellow players, Lajoie allegedly was allowed vital hits by a cooperative St. Louis Browns team, who played a deep infield and thus surrendered seven bunt singles to the Cleveland star in a season-ending doubleheader. Lajoie fell just short of Cobb, .384 to .385, but as a result of the charge that the Browns had aided Lajoie, the contest appeared tainted, so both players were awarded new cars. Nearly 70 years later, it was discovered that Cobb's hits total had been mistakenly padded by a scorekeeping error and that Lajoie had actually won the batting race.

Unlike most of the other ballplayers in "Lineup," **Christy Mathewson** was a college student when he was scouted for the majors. "Matty" was the epitome of a scholar-athlete at Pennsylvania's Bucknell University, serving as class president and playing three sports. He was especially outstanding on the football field, where he played fullback and kicked field goals. Smart, tall, blue-eyed, and broad-shouldered, Mathewson would later be called "the knightliest" of baseball stars by famed sportswriter Grantland Rice.

Mathewson's first few seasons as a baseball big-leaguer were bumpy ones. He was signed by New York in 1900, released after several disappointing performances, signed by Cincinnati, and then traded back to the Giants. New York experimented with the young pitcher during the 1902 season, moving him from the mound to first base to shortstop to the outfield. Mathewson's true potential as a pitcher was finally realized after John McGraw took over as the Giants' manager. From 1903 to 1905, Mathewson led the league

in strikeouts while winning 30 or more games each year. About a dozen times a game, he unleashed a special pitch that he called a "fadeaway" (which would later be called a screwball) that bent in the opposite direction of a curveball and left batters shaking their heads. Yet Mathewson's sensational pitching was based largely on his pinpoint control, and he was capable of shutting down a batter with any number of pitches. "Anybody's best pitch is the one the batters aren't hitting that day," he famously said. With Matty leading their pitching rotation, the Giants reached the World Series four times, winning it in 1905.

In 1918, at the age of 38, Mathewson enlisted in the U.S. Army after America entered World War I, effectively ending his baseball career. He was exposed to poison gas while in France, which caused him to contract tuberculosis. The disease took his life in 1925.

N is for Newsom,
Bobo's favorite kin.
You ask how he's here,
He talked himself in.

★ Louis Norman Newsom
Position: Pitcher   Major-League Seasons: 1929–30,
1932, 1934–48, 1952–53
Teams: Brooklyn Robins/Dodgers, Chicago Cubs,
St. Louis Browns, Washington Senators, Boston Red
Sox, Detroit Tigers, Philadelphia Athletics, New York
Yankees, New York Giants
Batted: Right   Threw: Right
Height: 6-foot-3   Weight: 200 pounds
Career Numbers: 211 wins, 222 losses, 3.98 ERA

★ Melvin Thomas Ott
Position: Right Fielder   Major-League Seasons: 1926–47
Team: New York Giants
Batted: Left   Threw: Right
Height: 5-foot-9   Weight: 170 pounds
Career Numbers: .304 BA, 511 HR, 1,860 RBI

O is for Ott
Of the restless right foot.
When he leaned on the pellet,
The pellet stayed put.

P is for Plank,
The arm of the A's;
When he tangled with Matty
Games lasted for days.

★ Edward Stewart Plank
Position: Pitcher
Major-League Seasons: 1901–17   Teams: Philadelphia
Athletics, St. Louis Terriers, St. Louis Browns
Batted: Left   Threw: Left
Height: 5-foot-11   Weight: 175 pounds
Career Numbers: 326 wins, 194 losses, 2.35 ERA

Q is for Don Quixote
Cornelius Mack;
Neither Yankees nor years
Can halt his attack.

★ Cornelius Alexander McGillicuddy
Positions: Catcher, Manager   Major-League Seasons:
1886–96 (as player); 1894–96, 1901–50 (as manager)
Teams: Washington Nationals, Buffalo Bisons, Pittsburgh
Pirates, Philadelphia Athletics
Batted: Right   Threw: Right
Height: 6-foot-1   Weight: 150 pounds
Managerial Numbers: 3,731 wins, 3,948 losses,
5 world championships

Surely the most eccentric player in this "Lineup," if not in all of baseball, **Bobo Newsom** combined outstanding talent with a wackiness that kept him drifting throughout both major leagues like a tumbleweed. In a career that spanned more than 20 years, he played for 9 different franchises, some more than once. This wandering allowed him to liberally spread his talent for perplexing batters and exasperating managers. Newsom referred to himself in the third person as "Bobo" ... but he called everyone else "Bobo," too. Some have suggested this was because he never stayed anywhere long enough to learn actual names.

As Bobo bounced from team to team, he earned a reputation as a competitor who would pitch through injury or weariness, sometimes starting three or four games a week and twice pitching both ends of a doubleheader. Once, when Newsom was with Washington and president Franklin D. Roosevelt was in attendance, Bobo was hit in the face by a bad throw that broke his jaw in two places. Asked if he could still play, Newsom replied, "Listen, when the president of the United States of America comes to see old Bobo pitch, old Bobo ain't going to let him down." He pitched a shutout for the Senators that day. Another time, Newsom completed a game in which a batted ball shot straight back to the mound and caromed off his head; he later said how much he enjoyed the music he heard through the remainder of the game.

Yet for all his light-heartedness, Newsom seemed to operate under something of a dark cloud. He once pitched 9 innings of no-hit ball, only to lose the game in the 10th inning. He was 1 of only 2 pitchers to win more than 200 games (211) yet lose even more (222), and he won 20 or more games in a season 3 times yet also led the league 4 times in losses.

★

Mel Ott kicked off his baseball career as a teenager playing for a semi-pro team in Louisiana. Brought to the attention of Giants manager John McGraw, Ott signed a big-league contract in 1926 when he was only 16 years old. McGraw played the youngster sparingly until 1928, when he turned Ott loose on an unsuspecting baseball world. That year, Ott hit 18 dingers. The next year, he belted 42. He did so using a batting style that was remarkably curious yet so effective that McGraw forbade his coaches to change it. As the ball came toward home, Ott lifted his front foot high in the air—a style described as a "foot in the bucket"—before driving into the pitch with an uppercut motion.

Ott drew an inordinate number of walks during his career (leading the National League six times), both because of his keen eye and because opposing teams feared his bat and therefore often walked him intentionally. The fact that Ott was freely given first base on a regular basis certainly cut down on the number of home run titles he might have won (he still took the league crown 6 times) as he accrued the nonetheless incredible career total of 511 round-trippers. By the end of his playing days, he was regarded as a double rarity—both the smallest of the game's all-time great sluggers and a star who spent each of his 22 seasons with the same team. When he hung up his spikes and racked his bat for the final time, Ott did so having cleared the fences more times than anyone in history except Babe Ruth and Jimmie Foxx.

Known as one of the sport's true gentlemen, the man called "Master Melvin" managed the Giants while still a player from 1942 to 1947. He later worked as a baseball broadcaster until his death in an automobile accident in 1958. "When he died," noted sportswriter Arnold Hano, "he held 14 baseball records, a little man with a bashful smile and a silken swing, baseball's legendary nice guy."

In 1901, Athletics manager Connie Mack signed **Eddie Plank** on the advice of the coach of Gettysburg College, for whom the teenager was playing. It proved a hot tip, as "Gettysburg Eddie" quickly became a standout pitcher with a side-armed, sweeping curveball that stymied opponents. Athletics star second baseman Eddie Collins once said of him, "Plank was not the fastest, not the trickiest, and not the possessor of the most stuff, but he was just the greatest."

Plank threw a wicked curveball and a good fastball, but his strength was never pinpoint accuracy. He led the AL in shutouts in 1907 and 1911 but also often ranked among the league leaders in walks allowed. Plank's secret weapon—and the trait that truly set him apart from the competition—was a stalling delivery that left batters in the dust. Writer Kirk Robinson explained it thus: "With a batter waiting at the plate, Plank would move an inch forward on the mound, then half an inch back…. When he finally felt the situation was right, he'd pitch, and not a second sooner. When it was wrong … he'd start over. An inch backwards. Three inches to the side. At other times, he would just stand and stare … until the spirit moved him. He'd just stand there. He'd wait so long that batters forgot where they were. Their eyes would water. They'd wonder about their contract, their girl in the next town, the weather on Venus. They'd wonder whether or not Plank had finally succumbed to some kind of cataleptic fit. And then the ball would be behind them. Strike one."

R is for Ruth.

To tell you the truth,

There's no more to be said,

Just R is for Ruth.

★ George Herman Ruth
Positions: Pitcher, Right Fielder
Major-League Seasons: 1914–35
Teams: Boston Red Sox, New York Yankees, Boston Braves
Batted: Left   Threw: Left
Height: 6-foot-2   Weight: 215 pounds
Career Numbers: .342 BA, 714 HR, 2,213 RBI

S is for Speaker,
Swift center-field tender;
When the ball saw him
coming,
It yelled, "I surrender."

Tristram E. Speaker
Position: Center Fielder   Major-League Seasons: 1907–28
Teams: Boston Americans/Red Sox, Cleveland Indians,
Washington Senators, Philadelphia Athletics
Batted: Left   Threw: Left
Height: 5-foot-11   Weight: 193 pounds
Career Numbers: .345 BA, 117 HR, 1,529 RBI

T is for Terry,
The Giant from Memphis,
Whose .400 average
You can't overemphis.

★ William Harold Terry
Position: First Baseman   Major-League Seasons: 1923–36
Team: New York Giants
Batted: Left   Threw: Left
Height: 6-foot-1   Weight: 200 pounds
Career Numbers: .341 BA, 154 HR, 1,078 RBI

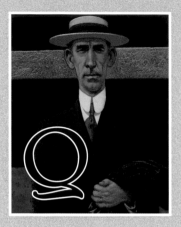

Nicknamed "The Tall Tactician" and "The Grand Old Man of Baseball," **Cornelius McGillicuddy** was most often addressed by his players as "Mr. Mack" out of respect. Sportswriter Red Smith once wrote, "Connie entered the game when it was a game for roughnecks. He saw it become respectable, he lived to be a symbol of its integrity, and he enjoyed every minute of it."

The son of Irish immigrants, Connie Mack signed on as a catcher with the Nationals in 1886, marking the start of a major-league baseball career that would span seven decades. He served as player/manager in Pittsburgh from 1894 to 1896, and in 1901, he became manager, treasurer, and part-owner of the new American League's Philadelphia Athletics; he would remain manager until his retirement in 1950, when he was 87 years old. As skipper, Mack set records that still stand—most wins, losses, and games managed in major-league history. His Athletics were frequently a powerhouse, winning five World Series championships and capturing nine AL pennants.

Lean and soft-spoken, the Tall Tactician was always circumspectly attired in a business suit, even when commanding his team from Philadelphia's dugout. Mack was respected by every player and coach in the game, including those of contrary dispositions. Ty Cobb, who played his last big-league season for Mack's Athletics in 1928, once told *The New York Times*, "I shall never forget Connie Mack's gentleness and gentility."

Babe Ruth. The larger-than-life "Sultan of Swat." Barrel chest. Matchstick legs. 714 home runs.

Just R is for Ruth.

Tris Speaker could have been inducted into the Hall of Fame solely for his hitting. He drove runs home in bunches, and in 1916, he ended Ty Cobb's nine-year run of consecutive batting titles by out-hitting "The Georgia Peach" .386 to .371. It was Speaker's work with a glove, though, that became his calling card. He played a shallow center field, swooping in on balls before they could fall for hits. That opportunistic style, plus Speaker's prematurely silvered hair, led to his nickname, "The Grey Eagle." The Eagle's unique positioning enabled him to pull off unassisted double-plays six times in his career, catching line drives on the run and then beating base

runners to second base.

In Boston, Speaker contributed to two World Series championships (1912 and 1915). Then, assuming the role of player/manager in Cleveland, Speaker led the Indians to victory in the 1920 World Series versus the Chicago White Sox. The final game of that season featured a classic Speaker moment. Cleveland was playing Chicago, and Sox outfielder "Shoeless Joe" Jackson hit a long drive to deep right-center. At a full sprint, Speaker leaped and snared the ball before slamming into the concrete outfield wall. The impact knocked the Grey Eagle unconscious, but his glove held the ball tight.

Speaker was revered by teammates and opponents alike. Red Sox outfielder Duffy Lewis called him "the king of the outfield," and Tigers Hall of Fame outfielder Sam Crawford noted, "I guess the best center fielder of them all was Tris Speaker. He played in real close and could go back and get those balls better than anyone I ever saw."

was no longer a pitcher, having moved permanently to first base. Terry was excellent with a glove, twice leading all National League first-sackers in fielding percentage. But he is best remembered for his impeccable work at the plate. In 1930, he batted .401, becoming the last NL player to break the hallowed .400 mark.

Terry was a gruff man who frequently became downright unfriendly when dealing with the press or team management. Of Terry's personality, Dizzy Dean once remarked, "Could be that he's a nice guy when you get to know him, but why bother?" Of course, this dour reputation may have come from the fact that Terry was not a colorful man by nature, nor did he indulge in the self promotion or late-night carousing of some of his peers. It appeared to many fans that Terry saw baseball as merely a business, but in his biography of Memphis Bill, writer Peter Williams suggests that this was so only because of his commitment to provide for his family. Terry bucked his reputation by producing a good quip on occasion as well. "I had great control," he once said, recalling his early days as a pitcher. "I never missed hitting the other fellow's bat."

As a young man, **Bill Terry** married a girl from Memphis, Tennessee, and pitched for the Standard Oil team in that city, thus earning the nickname "Memphis Bill." Terry made his major-league debut late in 1923 for John McGraw's New York Giants. By then, he

U would be 'Ubbell
If Carl were a cockney;
We say Hubbell and Baseball
Like Football and Rockne.

★ Carl Owen Hubbell
Position: Pitcher   Major-League Seasons: 1928–1943
Team: New York Giants
Batted: Right   Threw: Left
Height: 6 feet   Weight: 170 pounds
Career Numbers: 253 wins, 154 losses, 2.98 ERA

★ Charles Arthur Vance
Position: Pitcher
Major-League Seasons: 1915, 1918, 1922–35
Teams: Pittsburgh Pirates, New York Yankees, Brooklyn
Robins/Dodgers, St. Louis Cardinals, Cincinnati Reds
Batted: Right   Threw: Right
Height: 6-foot-2   Weight: 200 pounds
Career Numbers: 197 wins, 140 losses, 3.24 ERA

V is for Vance

The Dodgers' very own Dazzy;

None of his rivals

Could throw as fast as he.

W is for Wagner,

The bowlegged beauty;
Short was closed to all traffic
With Honus on duty.

★ John Peter Wagner
Position: Shortstop   Major League Seasons: 1897–1917
Teams: Louisville Colonels, Pittsburgh Pirates
Batted: Right   Threw: Right
Height: 5-foot-11   Weight: 200 pounds
Career Numbers: .328 BA, 101 HR, 1,733 RBI

A Detroit scout was the first to see star potential in **Carl Hubbell**. But the Tigers brass were troubled by his "money" pitch, a screwball that seemed to almost dislocate his arm, and gave him merely a shot in the minor leagues. Giants scout Dick Kinsella saw Hubbell throw in the minors and called John McGraw. McGraw had been a fan of Christy Mathewson's fadeaway pitch (a screwball by a different name), and when Hubbell was cut loose by the Tigers, McGraw brought him to New York. "King Carl" would never play for another team.

Hubbell posted 5 consecutive 20-win seasons, contributed to 3 National League pennants, and won 2 games as the Giants captured the 1933 World Series. But it was a year after that championship triumph, in the 1934 All-Star Game, that Hubbell staked perhaps his greatest claim to baseball immortality. Taking the mound to face the American League's All-Stars, he fanned five future Hall-of-Famers in a row: Babe Ruth, Lou Gehrig, Jimmie Foxx, Al Simmons, and Joe Cronin. Firing screwball after screwball, Hubbell punched out Ruth, Gehrig, and Foxx in 12 pitches, with a baffled Babe never even lifting the bat off his shoulder. Cubs catcher Gabby Hartnett, who was on the receiving end of Hubbell's throws, commiserated with his AL opponents, hollering to the other dugout, "We gotta look at that all season!"

By 1938, the torque produced by Hubbell's trademark pitch had left his throwing arm so twisted that the Giants star opted for elbow surgery. He came back but could not recapture his form, retiring in 1943. In the end, the destructive nature of the screwball did indeed catch up with Hubbell, but King Carl rode that dangerous rocket for more than 15 seasons and all the way into the Hall of Fame.

Dazzy Vance toiled for 10 years in the minor leagues, nearly wearing out his arm with his blazing fastball, before making it to the big time for keeps. In 1921, Vance underwent surgery and responded with such excellent form that he was rewarded with a ticket to the majors with the Brooklyn Robins in 1922. In Brooklyn, at the ripe age of 31, Vance won 18 games and the first of 7 career strikeout titles in his first full season at baseball's highest level. Complementing his punishing fastball with a slow curve, Vance would remain one of the elite pitchers in the National League for the next decade.

The 6-foot-2 Vance loomed large on the mound and delivered his fastball in a manner that made him seem even larger. He would rear back, raise his leg high in the air, pause, waggle his foot for effect, and then sling the ball home. He tried to enhance his dramatic delivery even further by slicing the sleeves of his undershirt into ribbons, but the league squashed that bit of showmanship. Vance's numbers dropped in 1932, and he spent the 1933 season with St. Louis—adding yet another colorfully named pitcher to a Cardinals roster that already included a Dizzy and Daffy (the Dean brothers, Jay and Paul). Although Vance suited up briefly for Cincinnati in 1934, he returned to St. Louis in time to be part of its World Series championship that year.

It is said that Vance got the name "Dazzy" from his favorite expression, "Ain't that a daisy!" which he pronounced "dazzy." As a man who embarked on his major-league career at an age when many ballplayers are looking at the end of theirs, Dazzy was a rare daisy.

Honus Wagner hardly looked the part of a superstar. His bowed legs, barrel chest, extra long arms, and huge hands made for an awkward appearance. But even though Wagner's running style reminded one reporter of a "propeller" and his fielding style resembled that of an "octopus," no other player of his time could match his feats at the plate and in the field. In his inaugural Pirates season, Wagner won the first of his eight career batting titles. Once he left the batter's box, he was exceptionally fleet of foot—hence his nick-name, "The Flying Dutchman"—and he led the National League in stolen bases five times. As a shortstop, Wagner simply had no peer, prompting Babe Ruth to remark, "At shortstop there is only one candidate, the immortal Honus Wagner. He was just head and shoulders above anyone else in that position." Ty Cobb called

him "maybe the greatest star ever to take the diamond."

Wagner gained fame among a new generation decades later as the star of the world's most famous and most valuable baseball card. From 1909 to 1911, the American Tobacco Company produced a series of cards featuring greats of the game. Wagner, who aimed to set a good example for his young fans, allegedly objected to being associated with cigarettes and demanded that production of his card stop. As a result, no more than 200 of the cards were printed, and fewer than 60 of those are known to exist today, making them a kind of holy grail among collectors. In 2007, a near-mint Honus Wagner card—a scrap of cardboard measuring one and a quarter by two and a half inches—sold for $2.8 million.

$\mathbf{X}$ is the first
Of two x's in Foxx,
Who was right behind Ruth
With his powerful soxx.

★ James Emory Foxx
Position: First Baseman
Major-League Seasons: 1925–42, 1944–45
Teams: Philadelphia Athletics, Boston Red Sox, Chicago
Cubs, Philadelphia Phillies
Batted: Right   Threw: Right
Height: 6 feet   Weight: 195 pounds
Career Numbers: .325 BA, 534 HR, 1,922 RBI

★ Denton True Young
Position: Pitcher   Major-League Seasons: 1890–1911
Teams: Cleveland Spiders, St. Louis Perfectos/
Cardinals, Boston Americans/Red Sox, Cleveland
Naps, Boston Rustlers
Batted: Right   Threw: Right
Height: 6-foot-2   Weight: 210 pounds
Career Numbers: 511 wins, 316 losses, 2.63 ERA

Y is for Young
The magnificent Cy;
People battled against him,
But I never knew why.

Z is for Zenith

The summit of fame.

These men are up there.

These men are the game.

★ *zenith, n. 1) the point in the sky directly overhead;*
2) the highest point; culmination; peak; summit.

Jimmie Foxx was raised on a Maryland farm, where he performed years of chores that undoubtedly contributed to his legendary physical strength. He played baseball in high school but dropped out of school to join a minor-league team managed by Frank "Home Run" Baker. Baker, once a star third baseman with Connie Mack's Athletics, notified his old boss about the talented youngster, and Mack had Foxx in an Athletics uniform by the 1925 season.

In Foxx's first few years in the majors, Mack played him sparingly, sitting next to him in the dugout and dispensing advice. Foxx absorbed these words of wisdom from "The Tall Tactician" and then shot to stardom. He was a monster in 1932, enjoying the best year of his career with 58 round-trippers and 169 runs batted in—numbers that earned him the American League Most Valuable Player award. Famed for tape-measure blasts that earned him the nickname "The Beast," Foxx bestowed a story upon almost every ballpark in the league. In Chicago's Comiskey Park, he crushed a ball over the double-decked outfield stands. A Foxx long ball in Cleveland Stadium won the 1935 All-Star Game. And in Yankee Stadium, he once sent a shot into left field's upper deck with such velocity that it wrecked a seat.

Foxx was a good-natured man who was extremely popular among his peers, but the sight of his digging into the batter's box unnerved many a pitcher. Yankees pitcher Lefty Gomez once said of him, "He has muscles in his hair." Added Athletics ace Lefty Grove, "Foxx wasn't scouted; he was trapped." The 20-year career of "The Right-Handed Babe Ruth" included 4 home run titles. His protégé in Boston, the great Ted Williams, said simply, "I never saw anyone hit a baseball harder."

Baseball fans today are familiar with the Cy Young Award, which is given annually to the most outstanding pitcher in each league. But most probably know very little about **Cy Young** himself. Small wonder, since the great hurler retired from baseball a century ago. In 1968, when Tigers star Denny McLain won the award after posting 30 wins, he asked about the man it was named for. "You've won 30 once," he was told. "Cy Young won 30 five times."

Born two years after the end of the Civil War, Cy Young came to the sport when the pitcher's box stood 50 feet from home plate. Three years later it was adjusted to the current 60-foot, 6-inch distance, and Young set records at both ranges. He broke into the majors with the National League's Cleveland Spiders in 1890,

playing the first of his 22 seasons. On the last day of that season, he pitched and won both games of a doubleheader. In 1901, the American League came to be, and Young moved on to the Boston Americans (later to become the Red Sox), for whom he would play until 1909. In his first year with the Americans, he led the new league in wins (33), strikeouts (158), and ERA (1.62). In 1903, the first true World Series was played between the Americans and the Pirates. Young won two games to lead Boston to the title.

Young's signature pitch was a fastball that moved like a gale in a cyclone (thus the name "Cy"), and in the middle of his career he developed what he called a "slow curve"—a pitch known today as the changeup. In 1904, he was in prime form with both, pitching the first perfect game in AL history. All in all, he threw 3 no-hitters, the last when he was 41 years old. He retired with 511 pitching wins, a record that almost certainly will not only stand forever but is likely to never even be approached. Late in his career, Young authored a list of rules for pitching success. Among them was: "A man who is not willing to work from dewy morn until weary eve should not think about becoming a pitcher."

My father's "**Lineup**" chronicles the names of famous players with whom he was familiar. It is likely that he saw most of them play, either when he was a little boy or later as a young man. To him and other fans of his generation, these men stood for the game of baseball itself.

Today, as we move into the second decade of the 21st century, new fans should make "Lineups" of their own—odes to players who speak to them and symbolize their generation. I know my father would heartily approve of such efforts and cheer them on.

–LNS

The Lineup

Grover Cleveland Alexander

Roger Bresnahan

Ty Cobb

Dizzy Dean

Johnny Evers

Frankie Frisch

Lou Gehrig

Rogers Hornsby

Walter Johnson

Willie Keeler

Nap Lajoie

Christy Mathewson

Bobo Newsom

Mel Ott

Eddie Plank

Connie Mack

Babe Ruth

Tris Speaker

Bill Terry

Carl Hubbell

Dazzy Vance

Honus Wagner

Jimmie Foxx

Cy Young

Acknowledgments

My heartfelt thanks go to Tracy Marchini of Curtis Brown, LTD, for suggesting this book to Tom Peterson of The Creative Company in the first place, to Tom for making it a reality, and to Aaron Frisch for his masterful editing. The searching out of the lives of these Hall-of-Famers has been a joyous enterprise for me, marred only by the fact that I wanted to write more about each one than time and space would permit. However, I heartily recommend that readers check out the online resources listed on the following page, which were so helpful in the preparation of this book. In addition, many public libraries hold wonderful books on these and other baseball players from the earliest days of the game. Two books in particular were of special help to me and a pleasure to read: *100 Baseball Legends Who Shaped Sports History* (2003), by Russell Roberts, and *St. Louis Cardinals: Yesterday & Today* (2008), by Bruce Herman.

–LNS

Web Sites

AbsoluteAstronomy.com, BaseballEvolution.com, BaseballHall.org (National Baseball Hall of Fame and Museum), BaseballLibrary.com, TheBaseballPage.com, Baseball-Reference.com, ChatterFromTheDugout.com, HowStuffWorks.com, Sabr.org (The Society for American Baseball Research)

Published in 2011 by Creative Editions P.O. Box 227, Mankato, MN 56002 USA

Creative Editions is an imprint of The Creative Company

Designed by Rita Marshall

Edited by Aaron Frisch

Printed in Italy

Library of Congress Cataloging-in-Publication Data

Nash, Ogden, 1902-1971.

Lineup for yesterday / by Ogden Nash; illustrated by C. F. Payne.

ISBN 978-1-56846-212-7

1. Baseball players—United States—Biography—Juvenile literature.

2. Alphabet books—Specimens. I. Payne, C. F., ill. II. Title.

GV865.A1N37 2011

796.357092'2—dc22 [E]   2010040121

CPSIA: 120110 PO1406

First edition

9 8 7 6 5 4 3 2 1